What Are Some Natural Resources?

HOUGHTON MIFFLIN HARCOURT

natural resources

soil

water

rocks

Natural resources are things from nature. We use natural resources.

clear water

cloudy water

We can describe what water looks like.
We can tell what color water is.

We can describe rocks by their size and color.

How can we describe rocks?

soil

pumpkin

We eat plants that grow in soil.

rocks

food

soil

We grow food in soil. We build with rocks.

How do we use natural resources?

recycle

reuse

dispose

We use natural resources wisely.

Identify Natural Resources

Help children recall some natural resources and how we use them. Then have each child name something in the classroom or around the school and discuss whether it is made from a natural resource and why. Then have them consider how each item could be reused, recycled, or disposed of wisely.

Write About Natural Resources

Write the following sentences on the board. Have children help you complete them to give examples of ways we use rocks, soil, and water.

We use rocks to _____.

We use soil to _____.

We use water to _____.

Vocabulary

natural resources   soil

rocks   water